Chain of Fear

**If you enjoy reading this book,
you might like to try another story
from the MAMMOTH READ series:**

Hazel Townson

Chain of Fear

Illustrated by
Harmen van Straaten

Mammoth

First published in Great Britain in 1998 by Mammoth
an imprint of Reed International Books Limited
Michelin House, 81 Fulham Road, London SW3 6RB

ISBN 0 7497 2885 X

10 9 8 7 6 5 4 3 2 1

A CIP catalogue record for this book is
available from the British Library

Printed in Great Britain by Cox & Wyman Ltd,
Reading, Berkshire

Contents

For the staff and pupils of Park View
Primary School, Prestwich

Author's note

This is a serious tale about Stranger Danger, based upon two separate true incidents reported in the news. Some children think the world is not really such a dangerous place as they are led to believe, because the dangers have been greatly exaggerated by nervous adults and by people looking for sensational news items. Many children are bored and frustrated by the constant watch being kept on them and are starting to wonder whether this is really necessary. Is it time for children to insist on their freedom to lead more adventurous lives? Read this story and see what *you* think.

1   Face at the window

MEGAN SHAW LEAPT up in alarm. A man was peering through the kitchen window. He was middle-aged, rather rough-looking, with stubble on his chin and untidy hair. As she stared at him, he began to tap on the window, mouthing something she could not hear through the double-glazing.

Megan was in the house alone. Usually her elder brother came home with her, but today he was in detention. She had arrived home from school only ten minutes ago, and had just settled down in the kitchen for a quick snack before starting on her homework. Had this man followed her? Did he know she was in the house alone? Into her head rushed all the warning tales with which her mother and her teacher constantly regaled her. Don't talk to strangers; be constantly on your guard. She began to move towards the hall where she could telephone for help.

Then she noticed that the man was holding up a message on a sheet of paper

and was pressing it to the windowpane.
it read:

**I'M YOUR UNCLE DEREK FROM CANADA.
PLEASE MAY I COME IN?**

Now Megan hesitated. It was true that she
did have an Uncle Derek in Canada,

her mother's brother. He had lived there since Megan was born, so she had never met him. Still, there had been no talk of him coming to England.

Megan decided to telephone her mother at work. She was not supposed to do this except in an emergency, but this was an emergency. As she slipped out of the kitchen the man began to knock on the window again. It was a most unnerving sound, making Megan even more anxious to hear her mother's voice.

Mrs Shaw worked at the estate agent's office on the High Street, but apparently she had taken a client to view a house and was not expected back for at least half an hour.

Megan tried to quell her rising panic. Her father had died some years ago and the only other member of the family was her brother David. He *would* be in detention today, just when she needed him!

The Shaws' house was detached and stood at the end of a quiet cul-de-sac with open fields behind. The nearest neighbour was Mrs Jameson, an elderly lady who lived alone and was rather deaf. No help there. The other neighbours Megan knew would still be out at work.

Megan sat on the stairs, remembering all the warnings which had followed her right through her childhood. Well, the answer was plain. She would not let this man in.

She crouched on the stairs, tense with fright, for what seemed like hours, though in fact it was only a few minutes. Then she noticed that the knocking had stopped.

That seemed even more frightening. For what was he doing now? Working quietly on the door lock, trying to force his way in? Or searching around for some heavy object with which to break the window?

At last she plucked up courage to peer carefully round the kitchen door. The man seemed to have gone. She ran through to the front of the house and sneaked a glance from behind a curtain. And there he was, walking away towards a parked car, swinging the car keys in his hands.

2 Thoughts of revenge

IT WAS UNFORTUNATE that Megan had no chance to explain. The moment her mother walked in, the telephone started ringing. Mrs Shaw answered and heard Auntie Rose bubbling over with the news that long-lost brother Derek had just turned up at her house on a surprise visit all the way from Canada.

'He did try your house first, since you're nearest to the airport, but it seems he couldn't persuade your Megan to let him in.' Rose sounded highly amused.

'Oh, now isn't that a shame?' cried Mrs Shaw as she replaced the receiver. 'I haven't seen our Derek for sixteen years. It would have been lovely to walk in and find him.'

'Well, how did I know who he was? Nobody said he was coming and you're always telling me never to open the door to anyone but family.'

'Well, of course, love! But he *is* family, after all.'

'Well, I didn't know that, did I?'

'You were quite right to be cautious. But

Auntie Rose says he *told* you who he was. He wrote it on a sheet of paper.'

'Anyone could do that. They could easily find out I had an Uncle Derek and use that as a trick to get in. Anyway, he didn't look anything like Uncle Derek.'

Mrs Shaw smiled. 'You've never seen your uncle.'

'I've seen his photograph.'

'Yes, from years ago. People do change, you know!'

'Not that much. This man looked like a real villain.'

'What, your uncle Derek?' Mrs Shaw began to laugh. 'Why, he wouldn't hurt a fly! He's the nicest, kindest man you could ever hope to meet.'

'Girls!' sighed David in disgust.

Now Megan turned furiously on her brother. 'And what's that supposed to mean? You're such a genius you'd have recognised him? Or do you think you're so macho that you could have dealt with any old villain, whether he was likely to murder us all or not?'

'Just listen to her! She's got more imagination than Steven Spielberg.' David aimed a scrunched-up ball of paper at his sister's head.

'Oh, stop it, you two!' interrupted Mrs Shaw. 'No need to make such a fuss. He'll come back and see us. Auntie Rose is less than an hour away by car.'

Maybe he would, but Megan felt foolish all the same. She slipped away to her bedroom and relived the whole episode. Maybe she had been a bit overcautious. Poor old Uncle Derek! Perhaps she ought to apologise to him? Tomorrow morning, which was Saturday, she could cycle off to Auntie Rose's and put things right with her uncle, face to face.

A detailed plan began to take shape. If she left first thing in the morning she could be at Auntie Rose's before anyone knew what was happening. She could talk to Uncle Derek, explain her point of view and invite him over. She was keen to meet him, anyway.

3 Accident

MEGAN'S BICYCLE WAS last year's Christmas present, and had hardly been used. She wasn't permitted to cycle to school as her mother thought the traffic was too heavy. She wasn't allowed to take it to the park, which was said to be full of undesirable people. In fact, she was restricted to riding to quiet local places, which she found pretty boring.

Well, tomorrow she would ride all the way to Auntie Rose's. She would leave before seven and be there in time to ring home before her mother found she'd gone. Mother and David would only just be getting up by then. She collected her things together responsibly: crash helmet, map, pump, puncture kit, water bottle. She studied the map with care, although she knew the way reasonably well, having driven there before in her mother's car. No one could say she was not being careful.

Saturday dawned bright and clear, a good day for a ride. Megan set out with confidence. The Saturday traffic was light so far, and she looked forward to a pleasant journey.

The first fifteen kilometres slid smoothly behind her and she really began to enjoy herself. Why hadn't she done this before? It was a real adventure, the sort that any young person could have had twenty years ago, before all this fuss about the world being an unsafe place. She knew that her mother regularly used to cycle six kilometres to school, and also to the seaside with her friends in the school holidays. How could the world have changed so much in such a short time?

Megan had reached open moorland by now. It was all very picturesque, and she

was just beginning to feel that this was
probably the best day of her life when the
accident happened.

There was a nasty pot-hole in the tarmac. Her bicycle gave a massive jerk and twisted sideways. Before she knew it she had lost control of the machine and was hurtling over the handlebars into a ditch.

4 Stranger in a car

FOR A FEW moments Megan lay face
down in the ditch, feeling shaken and
confused. Her bicycle lay in a twisted heap
nearby. Slowly she sat up.

Testing her limbs carefully, she decided that there were no broken bones. If she couldn't use her bike, at least she could walk. Then maybe a bus would come along or someone she knew would stop and give her a lift?

There was blood on her clothes which seemed to be coming from her chin. She put a hand to her face, finding some sort of damage there, but it didn't seem too bad. She certainly wasn't going to bleed to death, though she must look an awful sight. Would anybody recognise her in this state, let alone give her a lift? Her clothes were filthy, her jacket sleeve was torn and her face must be covered in dirt. She wiped it with her hanky which

came away blood-stained and black.

At last she hauled herself out of the ditch and moved unsteadily to pick up her wrecked machine. Regretfully she decided there was nothing she could do for it, and laid it down again. A sad end for a lovely bike!

But this was no time to start feeling sorry for herself. She sat down on a large stone to make some decisions. Could she walk all the way to Auntie Rose's house? Or should she keep to the shorter distance back home? The trouble was that before she reached home her mother would have realised she was missing. Megan had planned to ring home before this discovery was made.

Megan was still undecided when the problem was solved for her. A car drew up alongside her and a man leant out, asking if he could help and offering a lift. He was no one Megan knew.

Up until yesterday Megan would never have accepted a lift from a stranger. This warning had been drummed into her for as long as she could remember. It was one of the golden rules of safety. But her accident was an emergency, which surely must count as an exception to the rule and, anyway, this man was a clergyman; he was wearing a dog-collar.

All the same, she made no move but frowned cautiously at the man who had leant across to open his front passenger door.

Now he noticed the blood. 'Oh dear, you're hurt!'

'No, not really. Just a few bruises.'

'But your face is bleeding. And your poor old bike's in a sorry state! Where were you heading for?'

When Megan told him the name of Auntie Rose's village, he said he was going that way and would be happy to take her.

Once more she hesitated, all those long years of caution taking their toll. But the man did look kind, and he seemed so genuinely anxious to help. He had already produced a first-aid box.

'It's all right, really. I know you shouldn't take lifts from strangers, but I can't leave you here like this, miles from anywhere on a road with hardly any traffic. I'd never forgive myself.'

Two things finally decided her. First of all, she began to feel rather dizzy. It would be so nice to sit in a comfortable seat and be whisked off to Auntie Rose's. And secondly he offered to put the bicycle on his roof-rack.

'I'm sure it can be repaired.'

Well, that was a relief. She was quite fond of that bicycle and hadn't wanted to abandon it. So she finally found herself sitting in the front passenger seat of the vicar's car.

5 Sinister diversions

THE MAN TOLD her that his name was Michael Roberts. He said he was the vicar of a church called St James in a village she had never heard of.

In return, Megan told him her name and the reason why she was going to Auntie Rose's.

'I'm going to apologise to my Uncle Derek. He came to our house all the way from Canada, but I hadn't met him before and I wouldn't let him in. You get so mixed up sometimes that you can't tell good people from bad ones,' she confessed.

He agreed that she was quite right to be cautious. The world was full of unscrupulous characters. He approved of all the warnings given to young people, and he himself would not have stopped to speak to her today, except that she was so obviously in trouble and far from any other source of help.

They drove along, chatting pleasantly about school and the weather and the stunning view. Then suddenly the vicar gave a startled exclamation and, without any further warning, he pulled off the main road on to a bumpy little side lane which was scarcely more than a dirt track.

'You said we were going straight to my

auntie's,' Megan protested instantly, sitting bolt upright in her seat.

'Yes, I did, but this will only take a few seconds. You see, for over a week now I've been looking for a certain cottage, and I think I've just spotted it at the end of this track. I'm not going to stop there; I just want to check if it's the place I'm looking for, then I can come back later.'

Megan suddenly felt cold. She had been wrong after all to get into this car and put her trust in a dog-collar. Anybody could put one on and pretend to be a vicar. Even if this man really was a vicar, he might still be dangerous.

'Let me explain about the cottage, then you'll understand,' he began, trying to calm her. 'You see, it might turn out to be mine or it might not. My sister was hurt in a road accident and when I went to see her in hospital she gave me the keys to a holiday cottage which she had just bought. She wanted me to keep an eye on it, and to have it for myself one day. Then tragically she died before she could tell me where it was.

'I searched all her papers but I couldn't find a proper address; just the name of a place, which is Jasmine Bower. Any papers relating to the sale must be in the cottage, so that's no help. All I know is that it is somewhere in this county, so I just keep driving around, hoping to find it. Actually it will serve me right if I never find it, for I don't deserve it. Before the accident I'd quarrelled with my sister because she used to shoot rabbits; said they were ruining her vegetable garden.'

Megan thought this sounded a very unlikely story; the sort of story a man might tell if he were trying to lure somebody away to a lonely, empty house. A powerful sense of danger overwhelmed her. She wanted to leap out of the car, though she could see there was no chance of that. If only she had paid proper heed to all those adult warnings!

Then a woman appeared on the track in front of them. She was gathering something from the hedgerows into a basket. Roberts pulled up beside her and wound down his window.

'Excuse me, do you live at the cottage up there?'

The woman said that she did, whereupon Roberts thanked her and immediately began to reverse the car down the track and back on to the main road. All this happened so quickly that

Megan was still fiddling with her seat belt, ready to leap out of the car. She hadn't even had time to look at the woman properly, let alone think of asking for help.

Roberts was smiling ruefully. 'Ah, well! Better luck next time!'

If the house had been unoccupied,

would he have dragged her into it? One thing was certain; she wouldn't give him the chance to frighten her like that again.

'I'll walk the rest of the way, thank you,' she told him when they reached the main road again. 'I need some fresh air.'

'Open the window then,' he smiled, gathering speed. 'We're miles away yet.'

Megan's cheeks blazed. 'Well, I don't want to ride with you any more. Would you please stop the car and let me out?'

He turned, surprised at the tone of her voice.

'Oh dear! I've frightened you! How thoughtless of me. It was the turning off that upset you, wasn't it? I'm really sorry, and I promise I won't do it again. We'll drive straight to your auntie's now, even if we see my sister's cottage standing right in front of us.'

'I don't believe what you said about the cottage.'

The man turned to her again. 'Oh, I see! Well, it does sound a little odd, I must admit. But they say truth is stranger than fiction, and it really is true. All I can do is drive around until I find an empty cottage that calls itself Jasmine Bower. If my keys fit the locks, then I'll go in. Once I'm in, I'll be able to recognise my sister's things.'

The more he says about it, Megan thought, the wilder that story seems. She was now in a frenzy of impatience to get out of the car, but they were travelling too fast. Please let him slow down! she prayed, and suddenly her prayer was answered. Three sheep had ambled away from the moorland grass and on to the road. He was forced to stop.

Megan seized her chance. She was ready this time and, in one swift spurt of action, she unclipped her seat belt, flung open the door and leapt out on to the road. Only then did the sheep begin to move, shambling back on to the moorland, bleating with surprise.

The man was equally surprised.

'Hey, come back!' he shouted clambering out of the car. 'What about your bike and crash helmet?'

Megan ignored him. She was past caring about anything but her own escape. She ran away from the car as fast as she could, heading back in the direction of the cottage and the woman they had seen in the lane. Surely the woman would help?

The turning was further away than she had thought. What seemed no distance at all in a car seemed a very long way on foot. Worse still, the woman had disappeared. She must have gone back to her cottage. Well, that woman was Megan's only hope now, for she dared not accept another lift. In desperation she ran right up the dirt track and pushed open the cottage gate. She was so concerned with her own fate that she failed to notice the name on the gate, which was Jasmine Bower.

6 Shadow of a witch

JASMINE BOWER DIDN'T seem to have a doorbell, so Megan hammered on the door. She couldn't help thinking that the place seemed neglected. One of the downstairs windows was broken, and some of the glass lay on the tangled garden.

It seemed a long time before the woman appeared. First she lifted the edge of a grubby curtain and peered out at Megan. Then she opened the door just far enough for half of her face to be seen.

'Please may I use your telephone?' Megan pleaded. 'I've had an accident on my bike and I want to ask my mother to come and fetch me.'

The old woman stared. At last the door opened wider, a brawny arm shot out and a startled Megan was hauled into the cottage. The door slammed shut behind her.

This was hardly the sort of greeting she expected, but at least now she was nearer to contacting her mother.

'Please could you show me where the

telephone is? My mother will pay for the call when she comes to collect me.'

Despite her anxiety, Megan could not help noticing the mess. Although the furniture seemed good, the place was desperately untidy. There were dirty dishes, torn-up newspapers and empty bottles all over the place. Patches of spilt food darkened the carpet and pictures hung askew on the finger-marked walls. In her earlier panic in the lane, Megan had scarcely taken in any details, but now she saw that the woman was wearing a strange assortment of garments. Her tangled hair had obviously not been washed for weeks, and there was an unpleasant smell about her. There was, too, a wild look in her eye which awoke in Megan a new pang of fear.

'Ain't got no telephone,' the woman confronted Megan aggressively.

'Well, is there a telephone somewhere nearby?' asked Megan, edging nervously back towards the door. 'I need to ring my mother right away.'

'Oh, all right then, telephone's upstairs.'

Why had the woman contradicted herself? Perhaps it was just that she had not trusted Megan at first. But surely it wasn't usual to keep the telephone upstairs – unless the woman needed it by her bed, in case of illness? It all seemed very odd, but Megan decided it was worth taking the chance. She turned towards the staircase, every step of which had something on it: a heap of dirty clothes, a piece of broken crockery, a pan stuck with the remains of some long-forgotten meal. It was quite a struggle to reach the top, whereupon the woman, who had been following Megan, pushed her heavily into a bedroom and locked the door behind her.

Megan swung round in a panic, rattling the handle.

'Let me out!'

'Shan't never let you out!' the woman
shouted. 'This is my place now. My place,
you hear? And you ain't gonna tell on me.
Nobody ain't gonna tell on me!'

'I won't tell on you!' Megan cried desperately. 'I just want to get home. Please let me out! I promise I won't say a word and you'll never see me again.'

'Nobody'll see you again, that's for sure!' came the reply, followed by a spine-chilling cackle, then the sound of retreating footsteps as the woman made her way back downstairs.

7 Chase

HAVING WATCHED MEGAN run off down the road, the worried vicar climbed back into his car. The best thing he could do now was find this aunt the girl had talked about and raise the alarm. He drove as fast as he could to the village Megan had mentioned. Not knowing the aunt's address, he went into the post office and questioned the man behind the counter. Did he know a woman called Rose, whose Canadian brother had just come to stay with her? It turned out there were three women called Rose, any one of whom might or might not have a Canadian brother. But the man was not willing to give out any addresses.

Roberts was just about to leave when the proprietor's wife, who had been serving another customer and listening in at the same time, came over with the news that Mrs Rose Greaves, at the house next door to the school, sent regular letters to Canada. Thanking her profusely, the vicar hurried away.

He reached Auntie Rose's house just as Megan's mother was ringing up to find out whether her daughter was there.

'Oh, Rose, I'm so worried! Her bike's disappeared, but she hasn't left a note.

She's never gone off like this before. I thought she might have come to your house to see Derek, though she knows that she's not supposed to go off like that by herself.'

'I should have thought that Derek was the last person she'd want to see, after all that happened yesterday,' chuckled Rose. 'Anyway, don't panic! She's probably still on her way here. It's a fair distance to cycle and she might have stopped for a rest on the way. Give it another half an hour or so. I'll ring you back; there's somebody at the door.'

Rose was surprised to find a vicar on the doorstep, and when he mentioned Megan's name she turned pale with shock.

She invited the vicar in, and was soon hearing the whole story.

'I didn't want to scare the girl again, but I thought if I took you back with me and she saw that you were there, she would accept a lift after all. She really isn't fit to be walking all that way.

By this time Derek had turned up with an even better idea. 'Rose and I will take my hire car and go after her, then she needn't see you at all. We're very grateful for your help, but in the circumstances I think it would be best if we continued the search ourselves.'

The vicar was bound to agree that this was the best solution. 'Fair enough! I'll just unload her bicycle and helmet, then I'll be on my way.'

He handed them a printed card. 'Here's my address and telephone number. Do please let me know when you find her.'

Whilst the bicycle was being fetched Rose rang up her sister with the latest news.

'Now, don't you worry, we'll be out there in no time, and we'll soon pick her up.'

'Perhaps I ought to ring the police. Or an ambulance. She may have delayed concussion or something.'

'Stop panicking, Di! She hasn't got concussion, she was wearing her helmet. Besides, we know where she is now. All we have to do is drive out there and pick her up. Why don't you drive out to meet us? You might come across her before we do. But make sure David stays at home in case Megan rings.'

Rose and Derek drove off at once. When they drew near to the spot the vicar had described as his stopping-place, they slowed down to make a careful search, scanning the moorlands on both sides of the road. In this manner they covered several kilometres, and eventually met up with Mrs Shaw driving equally carefully in the opposite direction.

They all three left their vehicles and gathered together on the roadside to decide what to do.

'Well, since she's nowhere along the road, that means she must have accepted another lift,' Derek guessed.

'After all I've told her!' wailed Mrs Shaw. 'I must have drummed it into her a thousand times never to take lifts from strangers. She could be in real danger this very minute!'

8 Trapped!

MEGAN STARED AROUND the room she was in. It contained a single bed, a wardrobe, a dressing-table and a stool. But whereas the rest of the house was in filthy chaos, this room seemed to have remained unscathed. All the surfaces were thick with dust, but apparently nothing had been disturbed for a long time. The woman must sleep somewhere else.

The window badly needed cleaning, but it was just possible to examine the outside world. The room was at the rear of the house. Megan could see a wild, untended back garden with a wooden shed. Beyond that lay an open field, and at the far end of the field was a long stretch of woodland . . . a good place to hide, if only it could be reached.

Megan paced the room, trying hard not to panic.

The first possible solution was to reason

with the woman. Yet the woman seemed beyond reason. Maybe she was mentally disturbed. She could be one of those ex-patients who were often in the news these days, released from hospital with no relatives and nowhere to go. That would explain why she had taken over this empty house, determined to make it her home.

The second possibility was escape, but that did not seem likely either. It was a long drop from the window, which would not open anyway. As for signalling for help, the house was too remote for that.

Maybe patience was the answer. If she waited very quietly the woman might come back. Then Megan could be ready to spring the moment she opened the door.

She could take the woman by surprise, then flee. If this did not happen soon, then her last resort would be to break the window with the stool, climb out on to the window-sill and try to reach the drainpipe.

She crossed to the window, making one more effort to open it – and was terrified to see the woman emerging from the garden shed carrying a rifle!

Megan drew back from the window, her heart beating really fast. From behind the curtain she watched the woman cross the back garden carrying the rifle, and heard her open and close the back door as she came into the house. The minute that door was closed Megan made her move. She *had* to escape now, whether she liked it or not.

She picked up the stool and swung it at the window. The glass cracked but did not break. It took three more desperate swings to shatter the pane. The noise was terrible; the woman could not fail to hear it. Terror sent Megan scrambling backwards through the window, tearing her jeans on shards of glass. She clung to the end of the window-sill with one hand, reaching out in desperation for the drainpipe with the other hand, but it was just too far away. She could not reach it! That would mean she would have to drop to the ground and risk breaking her neck.

It was an agonising moment. Megan was not particularly brave or athletic, and she might never have found the courage to let go of the window-sill if she hadn't heard the woman turning the key in the bedroom lock.

Those were the worst few seconds of Megan's life. The woman had started shouting all sorts of crazy things and now she erupted into the room like a wild animal, crashing into furniture and knocking things over.

Megan let go of the window-sill. She felt herself falling, turning over in the air. She could see the window disappearing above and a great mass of greenery rushing towards her. Then came a sickening thud along the whole length of her body, followed by an agonising pain shooting from her left foot to her thigh. Everything went black, and she lay quite still in a crumpled heap.

When Megan recovered consciousness she could not remember where she was. Then, slowly, it all came back to her. The cycle ride. The accident. The lift. The escape and then the mad woman in the lonely house. She tried to sit up, but the pain in her leg was too great. Suddenly she remembered the rifle! At any moment now the woman could return and aim a shot at her.

From where she lay Megan could see the broken bedroom window, but there was no sign of the woman.

Megan felt sick with fear. Her whole life began to pass through her mind. She thought of her family and the good times they had together. She thought of her friends and teachers and the good, ordinary days of school. She knew she would never see any of those people again . . .

Suddenly a shot rang out. Megan jerked

convulsively and a terrible pain consumed her. She knew for certain now that she was dying.

9 An amazing discovery

MICHAEL ROBERTS DROVE back home to his vicarage. After what had happened he hadn't the heart to continue with the search for the cottage. He realised now that he had behaved very foolishly, although it was for the right reason. Perhaps adults ought to be alerted to Stranger Danger in a different way, realising the harm they could do with the best of intentions. All he could do now was pray for a message that would tell him all was well.

There was a letter on the mat. He picked it up without even glancing at the postmark, and stuffed it into his pocket. Then he went into the kitchen to make a cup of tea. He felt shaken and upset. Halfway through his second cup he remembered the letter. He slit it open without much interest – then leapt from his chair, sending the teapot flying.

The letter was from his solicitor, who had at last discovered the whereabouts of Jasmine Bower. He enclosed not only the full address of the cottage, but also a sketch map of where to find it. This was the very cottage he and Megan had driven so close to that morning!

Michael Roberts remembered clearly his first view of the cottage roof among its little oasis of trees, and his intuition was that this was really the place. His sister had loved the moors, and that spot was the sort of place she would have chosen. But of course he had turned away because of the woman who had said she lived there. Now, *there* was a mystery.

Suddenly a number of disturbing facts fell neatly into place. The woman must be living there without any claim to the cottage. So she could not be trusted, yet Megan might well have run back to her to ask her for help. Why hadn't he thought of this before? Feeling distinctly alarmed, he snatched up his jacket and ran out to his car.

It seemed a long way back to the cottage, though once he had moved from built-up area to moorland he drove faster than he had ever driven in his life before. At last he reached the turning into the rough little track that crossed the moor, and the dust rose around him as he bumped along towards the solitary clump of trees that shielded the cottage.

Parking the car just outside the gate, he rushed into the front garden, and was just in time to hear a terrible sound. A gunshot rang out at the back of the house – followed by a high-pitched scream of terror.

10 Bitter end

B Y THIS TIME Auntie Rose, Uncle Derek and Megan's mother had all driven off to the nearest police station. They knew nothing of the house on the moor, for Michael Roberts had been too ashamed to mention it. He had realised that, if he had not turned off the road towards that house, Megan would have stayed in the car and would have reached her family safely.

The police sergeant listened carefully to the story being blurted out all at once by three disturbed adults, but he was finding it difficult. Megan's mother was almost hysterical and the other two seemed to be telling a different story.

'Let's start again, shall we? We need a plain set of facts to begin with,' he explained. 'Now, if just *one* of you can tell me slowly and clearly exactly what happened . . . '

'But we're wasting time!' wailed Mrs Shaw.

'No, we're saving time. Just be patient for a few more minutes, and we'll soon have the whole thing sorted out.'

'Let me do the talking,' decided Rose.

At last the sergeant began scribbling busily. Then he made a few telephone calls and soon a search was under way.

But was it all too late?

Back in the garden behind the cottage called Jasmine Bower, the body of a girl lay twisted and still. Michael Roberts, running round the side of the house, spotted that body at once and threw himself towards it in a frenzy. He felt for a pulse, found a faint one, laid his jacket over the girl and dashed into the house to telephone for an ambulance.

It was then that he remembered that his sister hated telephones. Disturbers of the peace, she called them. She wouldn't have one in the house. All the same, he needed one so desperately that he searched every room, just in case she had changed her mind.

That was when he came across the woman, who had accidentally shot herself in the foot while handling the unfamiliar gun, and was bleeding all over the landing.

It was not Megan who had been shot after all. She had merely fainted from shock when the gun went off.

Two casualties and no telephone! Michael Roberts was now in a dilemma.

He fervently wished he had invested in a mobile telephone. How could he attract attention without leaving his patients? He was still searching desperately for a solution when help arrived in the shape of a police car.

The sergeant from the local police station had radioed to a patrol car on the moors to look out for the missing girl, and this patrol had immediately decided to check out Jasmine Bower, the only building near the spot where Megan was last seen.

Once the police arrived at the house and realised what had happened, they put out an immediate call for an ambulance.

Megan was soon sitting up in a hospital bed surrounded by four anxious grown-ups. She had met her Uncle Derek at last and the two of them were already firm friends.

Mrs Shaw gave her daughter an affectionate hug. 'Thank goodness you have nothing worse than a broken ankle and a few bruises. I just daren't think of what might have happened.'

'You needn't worry, Mum,' Megan assured her. 'I won't rush off like that again. If that was freedom, you're welcome to it! I've realised how hard it is to tell right from wrong if you don't know the people. The story I thought was impossible turned out to be true, and the person I thought was going to be the most help turned out to be the most dangerous after all. I'm going to be much more careful in future.'

Still, one good thing had come out of it all. Once the woman from the cottage was well again, she was to be given a place in a hostel where she would be properly looked after. What's more, the vicar had found his cottage, which they were all invited to visit once he had cleaned it out and spruced it up a bit.

The other three grown-ups nodded approvingly. They would certainly accept his invitation. In fact, they might turn that visit into a celebration party.

If you enjoyed this
MAMMOTH READ try:

Charlie's Champion Chase

Hazel Townson
Illustrated by *Philippe Dupasquier*

Charlie goes carol-singing to earn
money for Christmas, although he
knows his mother disapproves.

On his way he stumbles upon a
burglary and kidnapping. Charlie
finds a vital clue, but will anyone
take him seriously?

The chase is on, but only Charlie
can avert disaster . . .

Another gripping adventure
following the success of *Charlie the
Champion Liar* and *Charlie the
Champion Traveller*.

If you enjoyed this
MAMMOTH READ try:

Dead Trouble

Keith Gray
Illustrated by *Clive Scruton*

What a find! It was lying there –
just like the ones real cowboys use.

Sean and Jarrod hide the deadly
prize in their den.

Then Old Man Cooney discovers
their secret . . .

A heart-pounding adventure.

If you enjoyed this
MAMMOTH READ try:

The Stare

Pat Moon
Illustrated by *Greg Gormley*

Jenna can't believe it – just by staring
at someone she can make them do
whatever she likes! The results are
hilarious – not to mention chaotic!

Her best friend, Eddie, thinks it's
the most amazing gift – Jenna really
is telepathic. Then he discovers
the secret behind Jenna's
new-found talent.

But when he tries to warn her, she
just won't listen . . .